© 2020 by Kimberly Mucker-Johnson

All rights reserved. No part of this publication may be reproduced, stored in a retrieval system, or transmitted, in any form or by any means, electronic, mechanical, photocopying, recording, or otherwise, without prior written permission from the publisher.

Qui Docet Discit Publishing, LLC
Louisville, KY 40272
quidocetdiscitpublishing@gmail.com

ISBN 13: 978-0-692-43502-1 (Hardback)
        978-1-953376-98-5 (Paperback)
        978-1-953376-99-2 (E-book)

Library of Congress Control Number: 2020942796

This book is dedicated to Breonna Taylor, her family, and others like the main character, "Aaliyah" who have experienced loss due to no-knock warrants. This book details a theft of the soul of a young black girl.

BREONNA TAYLOR

JUNE 5, 1993 - MARCH 13, 2020

As of the publishing of this book, justice for Breonna has not been served.

"BECAUSE I DON'T HAVE A MIND TO DO THIS TODAY..."

On a regular, Aaliyah was a very social person. She had plenty of friends that she hung out with at school. And on a regular, Aaliyah did all of her school work to the very best of her ability.

CLASSROOMS

Today was different. Aaliyah showed up at school today but her mind didn't.

TODAY WAS TOTALLY

DIFFERENT.

The teacher kept wondering where her mind was because they had a test. Aaliyah couldn't speak about the whereabouts of her mind. All she knew was that her mind was gone. She just sat in class and looked at the test.

After several minutes of being frustrated, Ms. Baker finally said, "Aaliyah! Aaliyah, I need you to do your math test!" Then, she shifted her weight from one side to another, "You've done nothing today but stare off into space. What's wrong with you?"

Ms. Baker's reaction jolted Aaliyah. Aaliyah turned her head towards Ms. Baker, looked into her eyes, opened her mouth, formed the sounds but did not have enough energy to combine the sounds to make words.

Aaliyah's eyes were open.

Aaliyah's mouth was open, but Aaliyah did not utter a word.

Aaliyah had been taught not to discuss their business at school. All of this made Aaliyah exhausted, so she laid her head on the desk, closed her eyes, closed her mouth, and tried to rest.

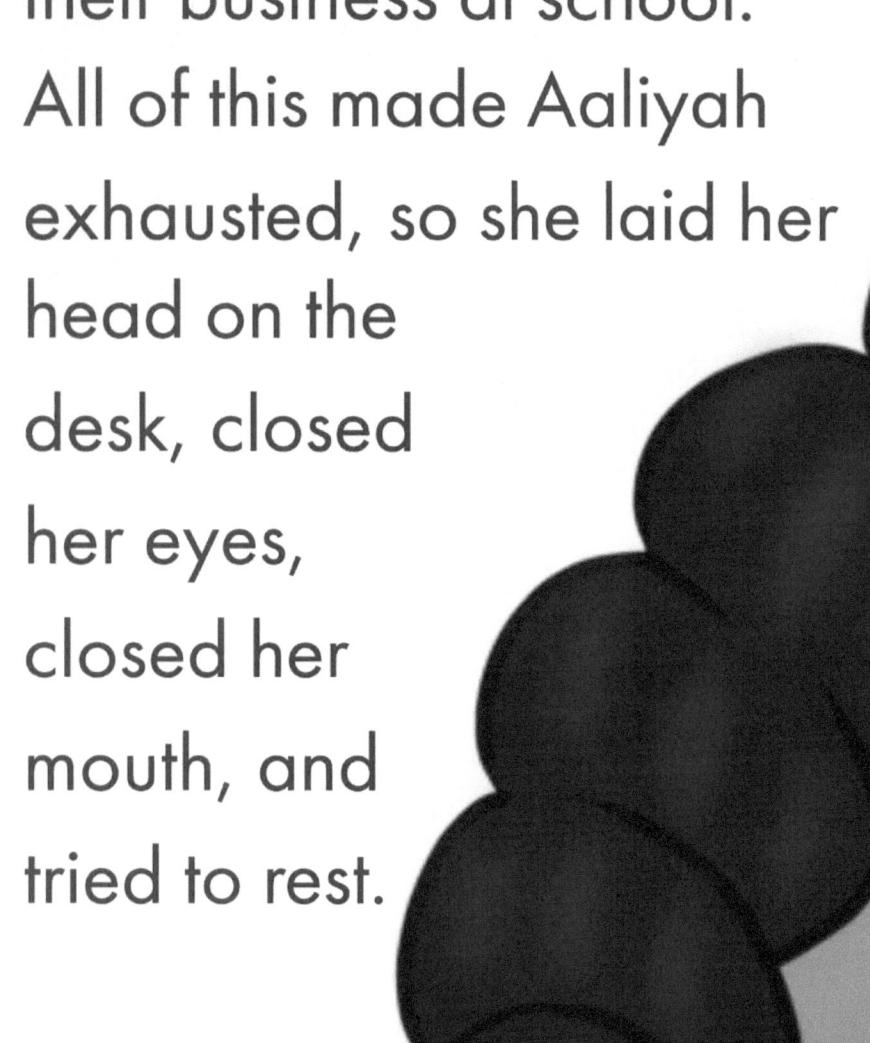

This angered Ms. Baker, "Get up, Aaliyah!! You're not going to sleep in my class!! I told you to do your math test!!!"

Aaliyah did not move. There was no energy to move. Aaliyah did not have a mind to move.

Ms. Baker marched over to the phone on her desk and called Aaliyah's mother. The whole class heard as Ms. Baker half-whispered to Aaliyah's mother about Aaliyah being defiant and refusing to do her math test. Aaliyah did not budge. She didn't have a mind to budge.

Ms. Baker listened to Aaliyah's mother for a few seconds or more. After a few "huh uhs", "ummms", and "oooohs", Ms. Baker hung up the phone and asked the teacher assistant to watch the class while she took Aaliyah to the counselor's office. She grabbed Aaliyah by the hand and said, "Come on, I'm taking you to the counselor's office."

When they reached Ms. Austin's office, Ms. Baker said, "Aaliyah needs to see you. I talked to her mother and apparently, her father was arrested last night. She's been uncooperative in class today. I just need for her to finish her math test."

Ms. Austin looked at Aaliyah's eyes. She scanned Aaliyah's eyes to determine if Aaliyah had a mind to talk. Aaliyah's eyes met Ms. Austin's eyes. Her eyes said, "I don't have a mind to talk." Ms. Austin told Ms. Baker that she would talk to Aaliyah and bring her back to class after they talked.

Once Ms. Baker left, Ms. Austin gave Aaliyah a piece of paper and a pencil. Ms. Austin asked Aaliyah to draw what happened.

Aaliyah drew this picture.

When Ms. Austin saw it, she was able to get some clue as to why Aaliyah had switched up or was acting different today.

Ms. Austin was a professional, so she knew just what to do. She sat down across from Aaliyah, so that Aaliyah felt safe. Then, in her most soothing voice she began asking Aaliyah some questions to get a full understanding, "Is the girl in this picture you?"

Aaliyah dropped hundreds of tears before barely being able to say, "Y-y-y-es."

Ms. Austin continued, "Who is this man holding a gun to your head?"

Aaliyah exploded.

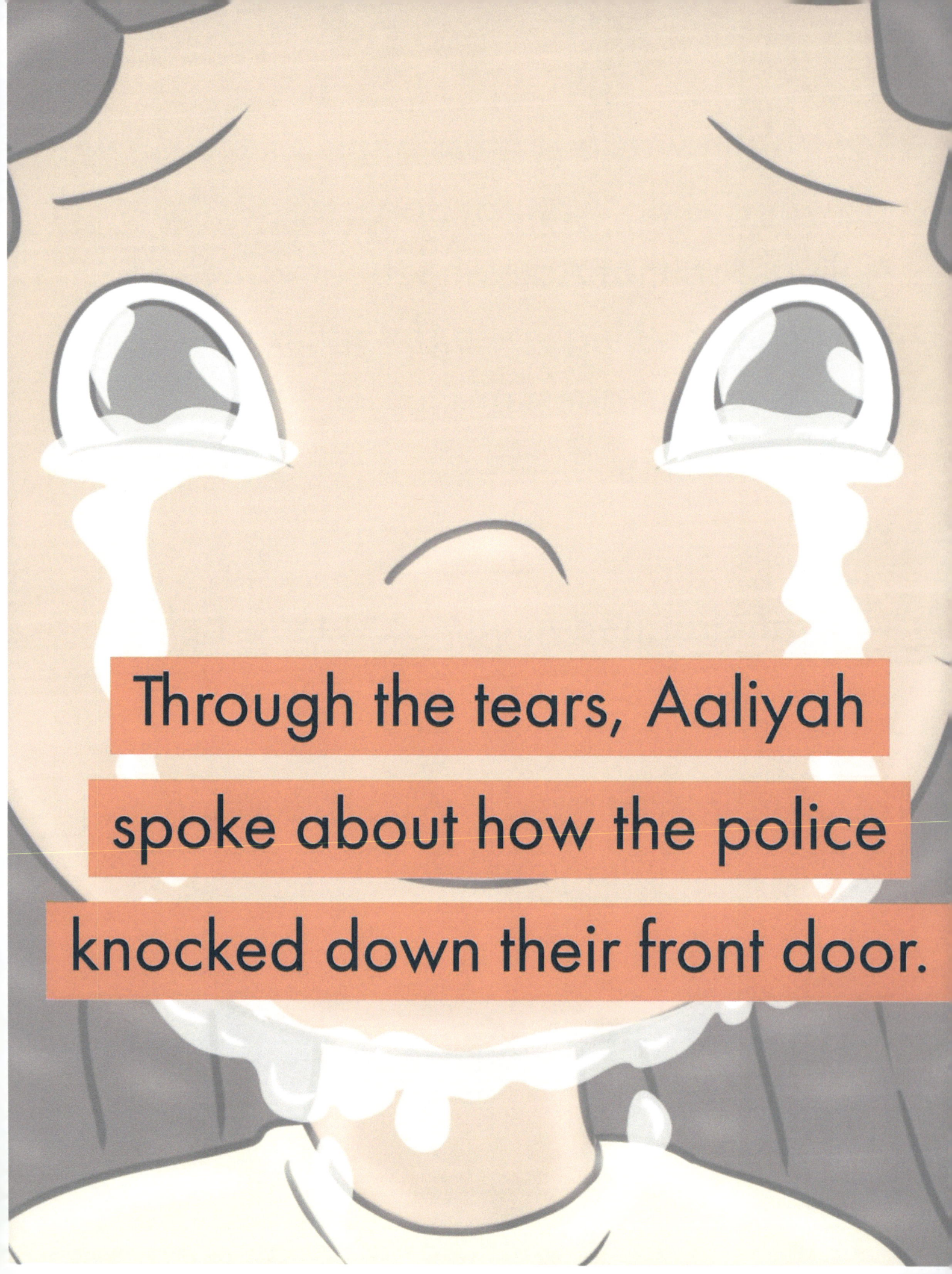

Through tears, Aaliyah said, "Everybody was upstairs and didn't know the front door had been knocked down. Then, we walked down the steps." Aaliyah first and her mother behind her. When Aaliyah got to the bottom of the steps, the police put a gun to her head. He put a gun up to her head "..for a while".

Aaliyah's mind left her. All she could remember was the front door was on the floor. Her dad was put in handcuffs. He went to jail. Her mother sent her down the street to a neighbor's house for a little while. Later, her mother came to the neighbor's house to get Aaliyah. They slept in the house without a front door. Aaliyah and her mother were scared without a front door. They didn't feel safe. Daddy wasn't there to keep them safe. Aaliyah's mother got her dressed the next morning and sent her to school as soon as morning came. Her mother thought she would be safe at school.

BUT TODAY AT SCHOOL WAS DIFFERENT.

AALIYAH SHOWED UP AT SCHOOL TODAY BUT HER MIND DIDN'T.

Aaliyah could not do a
math test that day...
nor the day after...
nor the day after that...
because Aaliyah's mind had left her.

Aaliyah had lost her mind.

Many times, people need time and space after something terrible happens to them. This loss of mind may last a few minutes or many years. Aaliyah was a very social person, and she did all of her work to the very best of her ability. Who knows maybe she'll never be able to find her old mind and return to her regular self. Maybe, she'll be forever changed by losing her mind. Maybe, she'll be able to find a a new normal..a new mind. Remember to always make room for others to heal.

Although Breonna Taylor is no longer with us, her life has changed and saved the lives of others by creating a more just and equitable community. In June 2020, Breonna's Law was passed. This ordinance bans no-knock situations as described in this story.

SAY. HER. NAME.

DISCUSSION QUESTIONS

1. What are some clues that someone may be hurting?

2. How can you get help for a hurting person?

3. How does Breonna's Law prevent this from happening to others?

Milton Keynes UK
Ingram Content Group UK Ltd.
UKHW050230200124
436369UK00003B/53